Magic Mommy Stories

Marvin and the Giant Bubble

by Karin McCay

Illustrated by Vova Kirichenko

Magic Mommy stories

"Marvin and the Giant Bubble"

by Karin McCay

Illustrated by Vova Kirichenko

WALDORF PUBLISHING

Dedicated to
Retief and Leizyl Ruby
because they listen with their eyes

Published by Waldorf Publishing

2140 Hall Johnson Road

#102-345

Grapevine, Texas 76051

www.WaldorfPublishing.com

Marvin and the Giant Bubble
The Magic Mommy Stories

ISBN: 978-1-945176-20-3

Library of Congress Control Number: 2016957004

Copyright © 2017

Marvin knew there was magic in her because whatever was terrible didn't seem so awful anymore when Mommy winked.

Whatever hurt didn't seem so painful anymore when Mommy kissed it.

And whatever trouble Marvin and Melissa Ann got into, even if they were in another room… or outside…

Mommy seemed to hear, see and know everything.

That was magic.

Marvin and Melissa Ann were about to go outside and play when Mommy said, "Here's a graham cracker for each of you. You can eat it or feed it to a bird."

They were barely out the door when Melissa Ann popped her graham cracker into her mouth. "Yum," she said as she gulped it down. Then, she said, "Marvin, can I have yours?" Melissa Ann could eat a whole box of graham crackers and still be hungry for more.

"No," said Marvin.
"I'm saving mine up here in my shirt pocket so it
won't get broken."

Marvin and Melissa Ann had a wonderful tree house in the yard, with a swing and a sandbox and a big slide.

As always, Marvin climbed the tree, and Melissa Ann ran to the slide. For a long time, they played together separately.

Marvin pretended to be a Superhero with a view of the world from the top of the tree house. Melissa Ann just wanted to climb to the top of the slide and watch how fast she could reach the ground again ... over and over again.

Then, Marvin noticed something
leaning on the bottom of the tree.

He hurried down and saw that it was a giant bubble blower.

He knew right away to dip the long, skinny wand into the tube and then wave it in the air to make bubbles.

The first time Marvin waved the wand, he made giant bubbles.

The second time he made
REALLY giant bubbles.

Then, Marvin walked over to the slide as his sister was climbing the ladder again. "Look, Melissa Ann, I'm a SUPER BUBBLE BLOWER!" he said proudly. She yelled down from the top of the slide, "Wait for me. I want to make a bubble too!"

But Marvin didn't wait. He waved the wand and
the MOST GIANT BUBBLE OF ALL came out at
the bottom of the slide ... just as Melissa Ann came
sliding down ...

And glub glub glub ...
That was the noise they heard when Melissa Ann
flew down the slide and slipped into the giant bubble!

And just like giant bubbles do ... It started floating up ...
With MELISSA ANN INSIDE THE BUBBLE!

She floated up ... over the swing set ...
up over the tree house.

Marvin was so proud of his giant bubble, he just stared in
amazement as she began floating away from the tree house.

That's when he heard his mom say,
"Kids, time for dinner. Come eat."

Uh-oh ... Trouble. How do you tell your Mom

The good news is ... I made the biggest bubble ever.

The bad news is ... My sister is floating away inside it.

Marvin tried to sound cheerful as he yelled to his mom,
"Just a minute. We need to clean up our toys in the sandbox."
That was true, but those toys had been there a long time.
Marvin needed time to think.

Then, Marvin noticed a bird flying near Melissa Ann ...
and he remembered the graham cracker in his pocket.

That's it! He took the graham cracker and with one smooth move, he threw that cracker as hard as he could and it landed exactly where he wanted it to land … right on top of the giant bubble.

Melissa Ann looked at the cracker on top of the
bubble and yelled to Marvin ...

"Thank you, Marvin, but I can't eat it ... because it's
ON the bubble and I'm IN the bubble!"

Just as Marvin yelled back, "It's NOT for YOU!"
The bird flew over to the bubble and snatched it
with his beak ... bursting the bubble ...

so Melissa Ann was free ...
but falling.

It was lucky that Marvin had on his fast shoes because he ran ... and ran...and ran to where the bubble had floated ... and then he held up his arms.

Melissa Ann fell right into Marvin's arms.

Marvin was so happy.

Melissa Ann was so mad, "That bird took my graham cracker!" she said.

Mommy yelled, "Kids, time for dinner ... Now!"

Marvin and Melissa Ann quickly cleaned up
their toys in the sandbox and ran inside.

They didn't say a word about their adventure.

But when they sat down for dinner,
Mommy said this prayer.

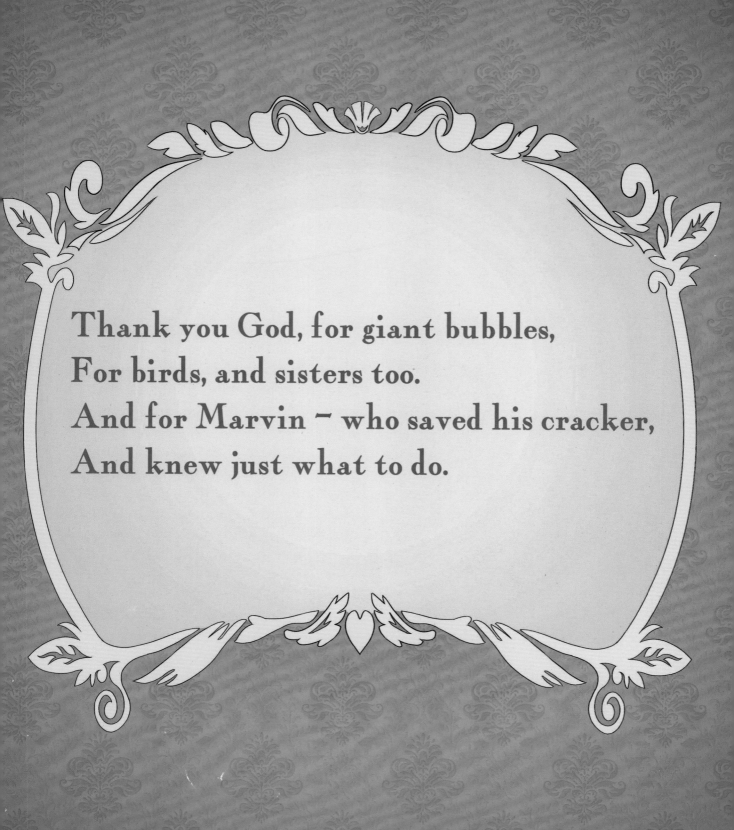

Thank you God, for giant bubbles,
For birds, and sisters too.
And for Marvin ~ who saved his cracker,
And knew just what to do.

Author Bio

Karin McCay is a 17 time Anson Jones Award winner, selected by the Texas Medical Association. Karin has won a regional Edward R. Murrow Award 4 times and earned a Lone Star Emmy for her documentary on the first South Plains Honor Flight. She has also received the Dean's Distinguished Service Award from the Texas Tech School of Medicine. Along with co-anchoring the evening news in Lubbock, Texas, she is a medical reporter and regularly contributes health stories to her newscast and on the web at KCBD.COM.

Since Karin and her co-anchor, Abner Euresti, are the longest running anchor team in the country, they have been featured many times in stories about friendship and longevity. The Lone Star chapter of the National Academy of Television Arts and Sciences presented them with the organization's Silver Star Award in 2009, recognizing Karin and Abner for more than 25 years of service in the industry. The two are also Ambassadors for the Children's Miracle Network, having co-hosted that Telethon for more than 30 years.

Karin is married to Bill McCay, a Lubbock County Commissioner, and they have two children, Morgan and Jacob. When Morgan and her husband, Daniel, moved to Germany, Karin began mailing stories like this one to her grandchildren, Retief and Leizyl Ruby.